THUNDERBIRDS

CRY WOLF

BY AISLING O'HAGAN

B🌱XTREE

CRY WOLF

It was just an ordinary day at International Rescue's secret headquarters until John Tracy picked up an unusual distress call on his global transmitter.

'Calling International Rescue...I've fallen over a cliff edge...I think my leg's broken...International Rescue...save me...Are you receiving me?'

John, pilot of the Thunderbird 5 satellite, was used to receiving Mayday calls from around the world, but this one worried him. It sounded like a young Australian boy.

'I'm lost, scared, please...don't let me die...please.'

John quickly beamed the alert back to base, where his father, Jeff, waited to kick-start the Tracy team into life-saving rescue missions.

'Good work, John,' said Mr Tracy. 'But did the boy say where he was?'

'No, Dad. Unfortunately he wasn't receiving me, so all I got was that he was trapped on a ledge and couldn't move. But he did stay on

the line long enough for me to locate him to within a mile.'

'That's close enough son,' said Mr Tracy. 'Right, Scott. On your way. John, leave it to us but watch out for further transmissions. You might be able to get a more precise fix on him.'

'Australia, here I come,' said Scott. And, grabbing the two wall lamps in the Tracy lounge, he activated the revolving wall which spun him round into the hangar of Thunderbird 1. 'International Rescue's on its way!'

At 15,000 miles per hour Thunderbird 1 took Scott swiftly to his location. Within minutes of circling the rocky area, he was able to transmit a clear picture of the distressed boy.

'International Rescue from Thunderbird 1,' Scott radioed back to base, 'I've spotted him, stranded on a ledge. I'm going in to land.'

Moments later, Scott approached the ledge but there was no one there. Then he heard a familiar voice above him:

'Gosh. You arrived just in time. You saved my life. What can I say?'

'It's OK, Sonny,' said another voice. ' That's what International Rescue are here for.'

Scott suddenly realised he was the butt of a boyish prank. 'Well, now I've seen everything,' he said, as the two boys came out of hiding. 'So you never did need rescuing. I think I'd better take you home and someone can do some explaining.'

Luckily for the boys, their father, Mr Williams, explained it all. He ran a small weather station nearby.

'I'm sorry, Mr Tracy. You see, life's pretty dreary round here. And when the boys' mother died I felt I had to make it up to them. So I made 'em these walkie-talkie outfits. International Rescue is their favourite game and I guess that makes you their heroes.'

Feeling sorry for the two boys, Scott decided to treat them to an experience they'd never forget. 'I've decided to take you on a little trip, back to International Rescue base, to see exactly what kind of trouble a false alarm like this causes.'

Tony and Bob could hardly believe their ears. As they climbed into

Thunderbird 1 they knew they were on the trip of a lifetime, bound for Tracy Island.

Once the boys arrived at the top-secret fortress the whole family, including Tin-Tin and Grandma, pulled out all the stops to give their two admiring visitors a great show.

Alan took them for a tour in the monocar to see the huge collection of rescue vehicles carried in the craft and John showed them the emergency transmitters in Thunderbird 5.

'Now we really understand why we shouldn't call you out without good reason,' said Tony.

'Well,' said Scott, 'If you understand that then I guess the trip has been worthwhile.'

After gorging themselves on one of Grandma's delicious teas it was time to head for home. But the adventure wasn't over yet. Standing by a picture in the Tracy lounge, the boys were suddenly tilted back and thrown on to a custom-built trolley which propelled them into the cockpit of Thunderbird 2.

CRY WOLF

With Virgil at the controls, the rocket's red engines blasted at full power while an artificial cliff face slid down and two rows of palm trees obediently bent over to give them wing clearance.

'Hold tight,' said Virgil. 'We'll have you home in no time.'

Meanwhile, somewhere in the heart of a Malaysian jungle, the world's foremost villain, the Hood, cast his hypnotic eye on a story in a local Australian newspaper.

'Two small boys...a weather station...Ha, ha, a likely story. This could be just what I'm looking for. And who'd have thought that International Rescue would be the ones to lead me to it!'

Evil and ruthless, the Hood always tried to be one step ahead of his enemies. For what the Tracy boys didn't know was that Tony and Bob's father was not running a weather station at all. It was a top-secret space tracking post, and the Hood would stop at nothing to get his hands on the priceless data it produced.

'I think I should pay them a little visit...ha ha ha...'

A couple of days later the boys were planning another game of International Rescue.

'Have fun boys.' said their father. 'But don't forget what Mr Tracy told you. Keep your radios turned down.'

Outside, while Bob raced ahead to hide, Tony rode his wooden Thunderbird cart and wobbled slowly behind, in search of another daring rescue mission. But he hadn't gone far when he came across a stranger in a jeep who said he was surveying the area.

'I've just seen your young friend running ahead into that deserted mine,' said the man. 'It doesn't look very safe. Perhaps you should go in there and warn him.'

'Gee, thanks Mister,' said Tony, charging ahead. 'I'll go and get him.'

'Perfect,' said the stranger in a sinister voice. And, pulling off his face mask, he revealed himself to be none other than the dreaded Hood. 'Now, I'll deal with those brats first, then their father.'

Taking a package from his bag, he hurled a small explosive deep

inside the mine.   The boys were thrown into the air and when the dust settled they realised they were trapped in a shaft and the roof had half caved in on top of them.

Alone on the Thunderbird 5 satellite, John was just beginning to think he'd had an easy day when an emergency call came through.

'International Rescue, you've gotta help us....This guy tricked us into the mine...He must have thrown in a bomb. Come quick...please!'

'Now hold on a minute,' said John, recognising the young voice. 'Is that Bob? Hey, we told you not to involve us in your games.'

'But this is different,' pleaded Bob. 'It's true, you tell him Tony!'

John was in two minds about the boys' story, but decided to relay the call back to his father.

'How do you like that,' said Gordon, sitting close by. 'A man hiding two kids in a mine and then throwing in a bomb.'

Mr Tracy sighed. 'I remember when you lot were kids, you had me believing all sorts of things. Now why don't we get some lunch.'

CRY WOLF

At that moment, Colonel Redwood, head of a top-secret space centre, picked up an alarm call from his mountain-top headquarters.

'Colonel, it's Williams...This is an emergency. There's somebody trying to get in here...I must get to my boys...You've gotta help!'

'Get a grip on yourself Williams,' interrupted a stern-looking Lieutenant. 'Tell me exactly what's happening.'

'I heard some noises,' said Williams. 'I turned on my monitor and saw a man out there. His eyes...he started to hypnotise me. He's outside now, trying to get in.'

Sure enough, at that very moment, the evil Hood was attempting to burn through the solid iron door of Williams' top-secret darkroom.

'Williams, we've just checked on your location. We won't be able to get help to you for another 3 hours,' said the worried Lieutenant. 'Whatever you do, don't let him get his hands on that material.'

'But he's practically through now!' exclaimed Williams. 'Listen, you've got to try International Rescue. They got here in 35 minutes.'

CRY WOLF

When John received a distress call from the panic-stricken space station, he lost no time in alerting the Thunderbirds crew.

'Of course,' said Mr Tracy. 'It all fits. Those boys weren't playing a game. They really are trapped in that mine.'

'Yup,' said Scott. 'Someone wants to keep them out of the way while that crook breaks into the tracking station. I should've guessed their father wasn't running a weather post.'

'Those boys need help,' said Mr Tracy. 'Scott, you go and look after Williams. Virgil and Alan - Thunderbird 2. You've got to get down that mine and bring those two boys out.'

Moments later, the supersonic craft were blasted from their secret hangars. Loaded with vital rescue equipment, they had only minutes to reach the danger zone.

'Remember what I told you boys,' said John from the satellite. 'Thunderbirds are on their way.'

'OK,' said Tony, looking up through the darkness at the fragile roof that was closing in on them. 'We'll be brave, won't we Bob?'

Alone at the tracking station, Williams stood, frozen with fear, as the Hood burst into his secret laboratory. He slowly slipped to the floor as he was overcome by the hypnotic power of the villain's eyes. The valuable photographs lay scattered on the floor.

The Hood snatched up the pictures and ran to his jeep outside. But he didn't realise Scott had touched down close by. In a hover-scooter Scott chased the jeep along perilous, winding roads. Then, suddenly, the enemy truck lost its balance, careered off a high cliff and was smashed to smithereens on the road below.

Back near the mine, Virgil and Alan landed Thunderbird 2, unloaded the rescue gear and went in search of Tony and Bob. 'Tony...Bob!' shouted Alan. 'Are you OK?'

'At last!' sighed Tony. 'International Rescue are here to save us!'

Using their advanced sound detectors, Virgil and Alan went deeper and deeper into the mine, and it wasn't long before they found the two boys pinned beneath beams and rubble. With no time to lose, Alan used his power-winch to pull them clear and carry them to

safety. Only seconds after they ran clear of the entrance, the old mine collapsed in a pile of dust.

Back home at the tracking station, Mr Williams was so relieved to see Tony and Bob that he hardly noticed Scott returning with the precious photographs.

'That crook didn't stand a chance,' said Scott. 'His truck spun off the cliff so fast, I'm sure it will be the last game he'll ever play.'

'Mr Tracy, I don't know what to say,' said Williams. 'You saved the documents. More than that though, you saved the lives of my boys.'

'Well, we were glad to be of help, Mr Williams,' said Alan. 'We should have known that the boys wouldn't break their promises.'

'Yeah, thanks again,' said the boys. 'But before you go back home, do you think you'd have time to check out our Thunderbird go-cart?'

Seconds later, Scott was thrown back in his seat as the small go-cart was propelled down a chute, speeding ahead out of control.

'The things we do for International Rescue!' Alan said with a grin.

First published in the UK 1992 by BOXTREE LIMITED,
36 Tavistock Street, London WC2E 7PB

1 3 5 7 9 10 8 6 4 2

Copyright (c) 1992 ITC Entertainment Group Ltd.
Licensed by Copyright Promotions Ltd.

Design by Root Associates Ltd.

1-85283-715 -2

Printed in Great Britain by Butler & Tanner Ltd.

A catalogue record for this book is available from the British Library.